The Snow Queen

CHILDREN'S BOOKS

LONG AGO IN A LITTLE TOWN freezing winter came. All along the chimney pots, over the cobbles and white rooftops snow fell soft on snow. Nothing stirred, except for the wind that whipped round corners and down alleyways.

In a grey doorway a ragged boy shivered. His name was Kay and he was all alone, his only friend a little flute that he played for company. The stuttering notes fell onto the air to be snatched by the wind and carried off. And poor Kay was pinched by the devilish cold

Out of the gloom two figures appeared, hurrying in the chill. It was Gerda and her mother coming home to light the fires.

"Mother," said the girl, "that boy looks so unhappy."

"Give him this," replied the woman, "but hurry up, Gerda, it's cold."

Gerda pressed a coin into Kay's shivering hand and its warmth comforted him.

The night grew colder still and snow swirled all about. From her bedroom window Gerda watched the thick snowflakes.

"They're like a million white bees," said her mother.

"Then there must be a queen somewhere?" asked Gerda.

Her mother answered in a hushed voice. "Yes, she is the Snow Queen. Her touch is colder than the devil's kiss. That's what your grandfather used to say. You can't see her but she's out there watching, where the storm is busiest."

Gerda shivered at the thought. She couldn't forget about the poor boy outside. When her mother left the room, she crept to the window, opened it and threw a soft white blanket down to him. Kay was grateful for this small kindness. He wrapped the blanket tightly around himself and settled down to rest.

Snow fell fast on snow and the boy sank into sleep. In the eerie silence only snowflakes drifted by. Then out of the dark flew a glistening sledge pulled by five white swans and on it sat a beautiful lady glittering like ice. Her skin was pale, her eyes were black and restless as the wind. She wore a cloak of billowing snow and she sparkled with bright jewels. It was the Snow Queen. She had come for Kay and beckoned him to come away.

Suddenly a bright light shone and woke Kay from his dream. The snow still fell, but the Snow Queen had gone. Kay felt a gentle hand on his arm, warm and comforting.

"Come inside," said Gerda's mother, "you can stay with us tonight."

And so it was that Kay found a home and lived with Gerda and her mother. Winter was no longer cold and dark but a magical world of white. Every day Kay played with Gerda, sledging and making snowmen. No children were ever happier than these kind and loving friends.

Until one day, when everything changed.

Kay was in the forest pulling Gerda on her sledge. Along the track were Pieter and Stefan, the naughtiest boys in the town. They had tied their sledges to a farmer's cart and were being pulled along in the snow. They mocked and laughed at the poor farmer who was innocent of their tricks. Kay's heart beat with excitement.

"Look how fast they're going!" he thought. "I want to do that too." But before he could join in their cruel fun, the boys sped past and were gone.

That night Kay and Gerda sat by the window. The snow fell like a thick blanket.

"I wonder if the Snow Queen is watching us," said Gerda. "Mother says her heart is colder than ice."

"I've seen her," said Kay. "She's more beautiful than you can imagine and sparkles like diamonds. When she comes here I will let her in, then you can see her too."

"You haven't seen her!" laughed Gerda, as her mother joined them at the window. "And anyway, if she does come, I shall melt her on the stove!"

Kay felt a stab of anger. Why didn't Gerda believe him? That night he tossed and turned in bed. "You wait, I'll show you," he thought angrily.

Suddenly an eerie light glowed outside in the darkness. Kay crept out of bed and opened the window. A blizzard raged and snowflakes pelted down, sharp like icy splinters. As Kay looked up one flew into his eye and he felt a searing pain. "There's something in my eye!" he screamed and blood trickled down his cheek. Outside, in the whirling flurry, the icy Snow Queen smiled.

Gerda, woken by the noise, ran to the window and shut it. "What's the matter, Kay?" she said to her friend but Kay turned on her in a fury.

"Leave me alone, you stupid girl. Go away and let me sleep!" Gerda was hurt by his vicious words and hot tears filled her eyes.

When morning came Kay's bed was empty and Gerda's sledge had gone. The sullen boy had slipped away and left the sleeping girl behind. Kay didn't want to play with Gerda anymore or join in her silly games. He wanted to laugh and make jokes of people, like his new friends Pieter and Stefan.

Later that day, when Kay was playing with his new friends, a strange noise came from the sky like the rushing of winter winds.

Suddenly behind the trees a crystal sledge flew past. A dazzling woman dressed in white looked towards the boys. It was the Snow Queen! Quick as a flash Kay grabbed his sledge and tied it onto hers. Pieter and Stefan watched in awe as their friend was whisked away. When Gerda came to look for him, she asked the boys where he was.

"He's gone," said Pieter. "He went towards the river."

High above in the leaden sky, the Snow Queen and Kay rode away to the North.

Far below Gerda called for Kay but there was no reply. All that was left of him was the little sledge which fell from the sky and crashed, unseen, into the silent river.

Soon the town was green again with the first buds of spring and the warm sun shone and the river flowed again. Down on the jetty a fisherman caught a rusty sledge in his net. When Gerda and her mother saw it they were sure that Kay had drowned.

The lonely girl wept bitter tears for her dearest, lost companion. She cried to the sky, to the birds and the trees to tell her if it was true. She even cried to the river.

"If only you could speak," sighed Gerda.

"I can speak," said a raven, perched nearby. "Why are you crying?" he said.

Gerda told the raven about Kay and how he had died in the river.

"He is not dead," said the raven. "I know, because I see everything."

"Where did he go?" said Gerda. "How can I find him?"

"Go north," replied the raven. "Let the river take you." And he flew away.

So Gerda climbed into the little boat by the jetty and set off along the river.

On and on the river carried her, away from the town and her mother. Hours passed and the riverbanks turned to meadows and ancient trees. It seemed to Gerda like a magical picture that changed as she drifted by. On and on the river flowed, leaving everything behind it and Gerda fell into a tranquil sleep lulled by its gentle rhythm.

When she woke, the boat had stopped at the end of a beautiful garden. It was full of flowers of every kind. Under a tree a table was set as if someone was having tea. An old woman came out of a cottage. She smiled as if she had been expecting Gerda.

"Now my dear, do sit down and tell me why you are here," she said.

Gerda told the old woman all about Kay and how she was looking for him.

"I haven't seen him, but I am sure he will be here soon. Let's have some cake," said the old woman. "I'll just go inside and get a knife to cut it."

In the garden there were tiny whispers. "Little girl! Over here." Gerda saw that a rose was calling to her. She bent and touched its petals.

"Oh, beautiful rose, have you seen my friend, Kay?"

All the flowers in the garden whispered at once. "We are the flowers that know the earth best. Your friend is not dead. He lies in rest, hidden in a palace, but he is not free. Hurry now, leave this enchanted place."

The old woman came out of the house and saw Gerda talking to the rose. "Come here!" she shouted, grabbing Gerda's wrist.

"Ouch! You're hurting me!" said Gerda as the talking raven suddenly appeared. With a raucous flapping the raven flew at the old woman.

"Run, Gerda, run," the raven squawked and they fled the enchanted garden.

Behind them the furious old woman gave one sweep of her cake knife and chopped the head off the beautiful rose.

Gerda ran as fast as she could, fighting through thickets and thorns in the surrounding forest. Bedraggled and bleeding, Gerda stopped for breath. The raven flew to a tree.

Gerda looked sad, but the king comforted her. "Do not despair, child, you have a power far greater than hers," he said. "It comes from your heart. Your love is that of an innocent child and no dark power is mightier than that."

Gerda did not understand what the king meant but she was too tired to think and lay down to rest.

The next morning the princess gave Gerda her best fur cape and boots. The king ordered a royal coach to take her on the journey. Gerda thanked them and set off into the forest. But the road was rough and the carriage rocked as it rattled over stony ground. The sky grew dark and storm clouds gathered.

As thunder rumbled, lightning flashed and the wild wind whipped around. The carriage came to a halt. Up ahead on the forest track lay a woman's lifeless body. Gerda jumped down from the carriage.

Suddenly the coach was surrounded by fierce robbers, and the woman sprang up. As she held a knife at Gerda's throat, a rough voice screamed, "Leave her alone, she's mine!"

Gerda saw that it was a filthy child who looked wilder than a tiger. She was the woman's daughter. Gerda was taken back to their camp by the robbers who drank and danced like demons. Gerda was very afraid.

"They won't kill you," said the robber girl, "as long as you do as I say. Are you a princess?"

Gerda said she was not a princess and told the robber girl her story. The robber girl felt sorry for Gerda. She was just a lonely child who wanted a friend. So when Gerda promised to be her friend forever, she agreed to help her.

"Take that reindeer," said the ragged girl. "He is very clever and will take you north. But wait until everyone is asleep."

So when everyone finally went to sleep, Gerda climbed onto the reindeer and held on tight as they galloped off into the night.

On and on they rode, through forests and valleys and hills. Days and nights came endlessly and spring and summer passed. Autumn fell in a flourish of leaves. Vast plains gave way to mountains and the ground grew frosty and bare. Far to the North freezing winter covered everything in white.

On and on they travelled until Gerda could go no further. Numbed with cold she collapsed into the snow. Then out of the storm came a lumbering beast. It grabbed the frozen child by her cloak and dragged her away.

When Gerda woke she lay in a room where a huge fire crackled and blazed. All around were oil lamps and fish that hung from the rafters. In a shadowy corner a figure moved then turned to look at the girl. It was the beast that had dragged her from the snow and Gerda was sure it would eat her. But instead the figure reached up and pulled off a bearskin hood to reveal the face of a smiling woman beneath. It was the Finland woman and she had rescued Gerda from the cold.

"Here," she said, "have some food." Gerda ate ravenously and in between mouthfuls she told the woman how she came to be half dead in the snow.

"Do you know how to get to the Snow Queen?" asked Gerda.

The woman looked a little afraid. "Not exactly," she said.

Gerda began to cry. "Kay needs my help. I must find him," she sobbed.

The Finland woman soothed the girl. "There, there, my child," she crooned. "I don't have the power to get you to the Snow Queen. You need the help of the Laplander for that. I can show you where to find her."

The woman unrolled a map full of strange markings and lines. She ran her finger along the lines, pointing to the markings, and told Gerda to listen carefully.

"Go north across the great river. It is a treacherous place, so be very careful. Then you must pass through the tunnel of sound. If you survive that there is a great mountain to climb. Beyond it is the land of the midnight sun, that is where you will find the Lapland woman."

Gerda and the reindeer pushed on through arctic winds and deep, relentless snow. After many miles they came to the great river and crossed the huge ice flow.

Exhausted and freezing, Gerda and the reindeer arrived at the entrance to the tunnel of sound. Inside they were deafened by screeching echoes. They fought their way through blasting winds and blinding colours. At last the travellers left the howling screams behind and stepped outside into the eerie silence.

There in front of them stood a vast mountain, its peak disappearing up into the clouds. There was no time to stop, so Gerda and the reindeer started to climb the mountain's treacherous heights. At the top they could see for miles across a plain of perpetual winter. All was frozen and white in the land of the midnight sun.

ARGUING
WITH A REDCOAT
You make a pair of shoes
for a British soldier but he
refuses to pay for them.
Many Bostonians are
mistreated in similar
ways by the British.

Handy hint
Don't argue
with British
soldiers
stationed in the
town, you
could be
beaten-up, or
even worse!

APPRENTICE SHOEMAKER   TOO SHORT FOR THE ARMY   IN DEBTOR'S PRISON

No taxation without representation!

I n 1763 Britain and France sign a treaty to end the French and Indian War. This gives the British control of Canada and makes the American colonies secure from attack by the French and their Indian allies. But the war has cost a great deal of money, and the British Parliament votes to tax the colonists to help pay for the cost of defending them. Over the next few years Parliament passes the Sugar Act in 1764, the Stamp Act in 1765, and the Townshend Acts in 1767 to raise money by taxing various goods. This leads to protests and the soon-to-be familiar cry of "No taxation without representation!" American colonists are not represented in the British Parliament, and they have no say in any of the laws it passes.

Taxing the colonists:

THE SUGAR ACT (left)
Many goods imported into America became subject to tax, including sugar, coffee, wine, glass, paint, paper and tea.

THE STAMP ACT (right)
Direct taxes were imposed on legal documents, newspapers, and other printed materials. 'Stamp Masters' were appointed to collect taxes.

HANG HIM!
An effigy of a
Stamp Master hangs
from Boston's famous
'Liberty Tree.'

Handy hint
If you want to keep your friends, don't become a Stamp Master!

BURN HIM! A mob burns down the house of Governor Hutchinson, who supports the taxes.

The Boston Massacre

Boston becomes the centre of discontent with British rule, so the British government stations 4,000 troops in the city – about one soldier for every four civilians. On the afternoon of March 5th, 1770, a group of boys begin throwing snowballs at a sentry guarding the customs house. You are amongst the crowd that gathers to watch the fun. When the sentry summons help, a squad of eight soldiers confronts the crowd and open fire, killing five civilians. You are standing next to James Caldwell, one of the victims, and catch the dying man in your arms. The soldiers are eventually put on trial but only two are found guilty. Their hands are branded – a lenient punishment that enrages all Bostonians.

What led to the massacre:

TEN DAYS before the massacre a crowd picketed a shop that was importing British goods (right). A customs informer fired into the crowd, killing an 11-year-old boy. His funeral was attended by over 2,000 Bostonians.

TWO DAYS before the massacre some off-duty British soldiers were beaten up by Bostonians (above). This angers the British, many of whom want revenge.

BOYS throw snowballs at a sentry who calls for help (above).

A CROWD GATHERS As more snowballs are thrown, the soldiers fire at the unarmed civilians (above right). Three are killed on the spot and two die later from their wounds.

CRISPUS ATTUCKS is one of those killed. He is believed to have been an African-American. Some historians view him as the first casualty of the American Revolution.

Sons of Liberty

hen the American colonists first protest against the new taxes, few consider independence from Britain. They simply want to be treated fairly and to have some control over the laws and taxes imposed on them by a distant government. But the Boston Massacre fuels a growing resentment against British rule. Citizens begin to band together to oppose new taxes. One group in New York call themselves the Sons of Liberty, and soon other colonies follow their lead and form their own Sons of Liberty groups. You attend meetings held under the famous 'Liberty Tree,' but at that point you have no idea where the cries of "Liberty!" will lead.

Means of communication:

HANDBILLS (left)
Printed handbills are an important part of the anti-British propaganda campaign run by the Sons of Liberty.

COURIERS (right)
Committees of Correspondence are set up to send messages between the American colonies. These messages are carried by couriers on horseback.

"Liberty!"

Handy hint

Don't get caught giving out handbills or you might be sent to prison!

SAMUEL ADAMS (right) is a Boston lawyer, and leader of the Sons of Liberty in Massachusetts. Adams is a firm believer in colonists' rights.

TARRED AND FEATHERED (left). The Sons organise boycotts of merchants who import British goods. They also harass customs officials, some of whom are tarred and feathered by angry colonists.

The Tea Tax

**A**fter the Boston Massacre the British try to appease the colonists: troops are withdrawn from Boston and all major import taxes are removed, except for the tax on tea. The colonists begin to buy British goods again, but not tea! The 1773 Tea Act removes the tax, but sales are controlled by "tea agents." This leads to cheaper tea, but the colonists still oppose the new law. You aren't a tea drinker, but you join the crowds at the Liberty Tree on November 3rd to demand that the tea agents resign. Fearing for their lives, the agents ask Governor Hutchinson to take over. By the end of the month the British tea ship *Dartmouth* sails into Boston Harbour.

The British East India Company:

TEA PLANTATIONS (right). Tea imported into America comes from plantations in India owned by the British East India Company. The British government wants its company to have control of all tea sold in America.

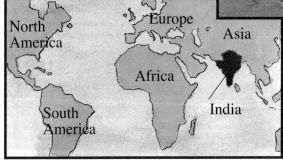

TEA AGENTS (right) American merchants are worried that if the British can appoint tea agents, they can do the same for other goods. This would mean that they could control trade and even ruin American businesses.

TEA DRINKING
Although all classes drink tea, it is a ritual in middle and upper-class homes where ladies serve tea in fine cups made of china or porcelain.

Handy hint
Get used to drinking coffee, tea is going to be in short supply!

15

A Growing Rebellion

With the arrival of the first tea ship, over 5,000 people gather at the Old South Meeting House to hear the leaders of the Sons speak. It is agreed that the tea must not be landed, and the ships should return to Britain. You are in the crowd and watch as two more tea ships dock in the harbour. The tea remains on board, but Governor Hutchinson has set a date of December 17th for the cargo to be unloaded under the protection of British soldiers. On the 16th, a huge crowd gathers, determined to stop the tea from landing on American soil.

How events unfold:

THE *DARTMOUTH* (above) arrives in Boston Harbour on November 27th, but the crowd prevents its cargo of tea from being unloaded. She is joined by two other British tea ships, the *Eleanor* and the *Beaver*.

GOVERNOR HUTCHINSON (above) is determined that the tea will land. He knows if a ship isn't unloaded within 20 days of entering port, its cargo can be seized. The governor plans to use this law, enforced by British soldiers.

Handy hint
Wear a disguise to avoid being spotted at the tea party!

OLD SOUTH MEETING HOUSE
(left). Built in 1729 as a Puritan meeting house, it is the largest building in colonial Boston. Important meetings of the Sons of Liberty take place here on November 30th and December 16th 1773. When he hears about Governor Hutchinson's refusal to let the tea ships return to Britain, Samuel Adams tells the crowd, "This meeting can do nothing more to save the country."

INSIDE THE MEETING.
Some are dressed as Indians, ready for the action about to take place that night. Roth arrives at 5.45pm to tell them of the Governor's decision. The tea party is about to begin…

FRANCIS ROTH, son of the *Dartmouth's* owner, rides to Hutchinson's house outside Boston to seek permission for the ship's return to Britain with its cargo of tea.

17

The Boston Tea Party

The Sons decide that the tea must be destroyed as the Governor will not let the ships return their cargo to Britain. Around 30 men are set this task, they dress as Mohawk Indians to avoid being recognised. About 100 more, including you, join them. Your job is to board a ship and demand the keys for its hold. The captains hand over the keys, and the 'Indians' lift the tea chests onto the deck. They split open 342 tea chests on three boats with hatchets and tip the contents into the sea. It takes three hours to complete while a huge crowd cheers you on from the dockside.

Boston Harbour is a teapot!

TEA PARTY SONG.
"Rally Mohawks!
Bring your axes,
and tell King George
we'll pay no
taxes on his
foreign tea!"

Handy hint

Don't steal any
British tea,
the crowd
might
lynch you!

Tea Thief!

You spot Captain O'Connor trying
to steal tea – which the Sons have
forbidden. His coat tears as you
grab him but he escapes and is
chased by the crowd.

Captain
O'Connor

THE PIECE of torn coat is nailed to a
whipping post to shame O'Connor.

Punishment from London:
The Intolerable Acts

hen news of the tea party reaches Britain, the King and Parliament are outraged. A series of laws (known as the Intolerable Acts,) are passed to punish the colonists. Boston Harbour is closed, the powers of the Massachusetts government are reduced and the colonists are ordered to provide quarters for British troops. The people of Boston are angered by this latest tyranny imposed from London and know they must make a stand to defend their liberty. But many loyalists still support the British, and you are about to encounter one of them!

A loyalist encounter:

YOU STOP John Malcolm, a known loyalist and customs informer, from beating a boy. He strikes your head with his cane, knocking you unconscious.

LED BY THE Sons of Liberty, a crowd drags Malcolm from his house and takes him to the Liberty Tree, where he is tarred and feathered.

REVENGE! Angry members of Parliament pass the Boston Port Act, closing the harbour until the tea is paid for.

Handy hint

Don't get into a fight with loyalists, you could get hurt!

'Mad' King George

KING GEORGE III (1738-1820) is the British monarch during and after the events leading up to the American Revolution. He supports the strong measures against the colonists, stating that "We must master them or leave them to themselves." In later life he suffers from periods of ill-health and insanity believed to be caused by an illness called porphyria.

The British are coming!

t is hoped that the Intolerable Acts will end rebellion in the colonies but they have the opposite effect. In September 1774, the First Continental Congress is attended by representatives from 12 of the 13 colonies. They protest about the new laws and urge the colonists to arm themselves to defend their rights. General Gage, now governor of Massachusetts, enforces the new laws and is determined to capture your leaders. Hundreds of British troops search the town for weapons. Paul Revere warns Samuel Adams and John Hancock of the British plan to arrest them. They escape, but local militia decide to oppose the British troops and fight for liberty.

PAUL REVERE (right)
A Boston silversmith and engraver, Revere is a leader of the Sons who took part in the Boston Tea Party. He is also a courier for the Massachusetts Committee of Correspondence.

REVERE'S RIDE (right) On the night of April 18/19th 1775, Revere rides 25 km from Charlestown to Lexington to warn other leaders of the Sons of Liberty that the British are marching to arrest them.

LEXINGTON

CONCORD

British route

Revere's route

BATTLES OF LEXINGTON AND CONCORD On April 19th, about 75 colonial militia confront 700 British troops on Lexington Green. Shooting begins; eight militia are killed and ten wounded. The British then march to Concord to destroy arms supplies. But word spreads, and thousands of colonists begin to converge on the town. Now outnumbered, the British make a fighting retreat back to Boston.

Boston Besieged:
The Battle of Bunker Hill

The British retreat from Concord spurs other patriots to converge on Boston from towns throughout Massachusetts and the surrounding colonies. By June 1775, American general Artemas Ward leads 15,000 volunteers, who lay siege to 6,400 British troops in Boston. On June 16th, 1,500 of the Americans take up a position on the heights of Charlestown peninsula, controlling access to Boston Harbour. General Gage sends 2,400 in British troops to force them out, and by the next day a pitched battle takes place. The Americans are driven from the peninsula, but the British lose over 1,000 men compared to 450 American casualties. The Boston garrison is evacuated in 1776.

THE MINUTEMEN (left) are a local militia organised to oppose the British. They are known as Minutemen because they could be called to arms at a minute's notice. You want to join them, but the British stop all able-bodied men from leaving Boston to join the patriots.

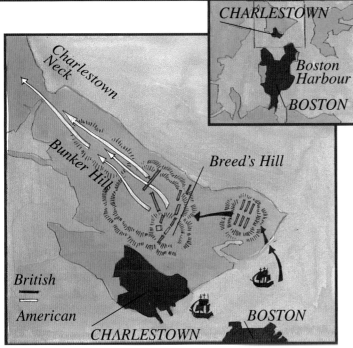

Handy hint

Throw away any red clothes, in case you're mistaken for a redcoat!

THE BATTLE OF BUNKER HILL (above) British forces land and advance on Breed's Hill. Two attacks are repulsed, but a third drives the Americans back along the peninsula. You watch the battle from across the bay.

THE REDCOATS (right) are so called because of the colour of their uniform. Many of the 'British' troops are actually German! King George III has German ancestry and up to 30,000 Hessians (from the German region of Hesse) are fighting for the British.

The American Revolution

he Battle of Bunker Hill is the first major engagement in what will become an eight-year-long struggle for American independence. General George Washington is appointed commander of the Continental Army, which fights the British in the northern colonies. The British dominate the opening years of the war by capturing New York and Philadelphia. But the Americans are now determined to win their liberty, and on July 4th 1776, the Declaration of Independence is approved by the Continental Congress. The United States of America is born, but the war continues. You escape from Boston in 1775 and meet George Washington, who is planning to recapture the city. You volunteer to fight and spend many months at sea as well as serving as a private in the militia.

BATTLES AT SEA Sailing from Boston, you fight aboard a privateer – a privately owned ship employed to fight the British. Boston is the centre of the American navy, and during the war captured ships are sailed into the town's harbour.

LIBERTY BELL The symbol of American independence, the Liberty Bell (above), rings out after the Declaration of Independence is signed in Philadelphia.

Handy hint

Join the navy, it's less dangerous than being a soldier and you may win a share of the plunder!

CROSSING THE DELAWARE On Christmas night 1776, Washington and 2,500 soldiers cross the icy Delaware River. They surprise the British and win battles at Trenton and Princeton. These important early victories boost American morale.

STARS AND STRIPES The 13 stars and stripes on this American flag represent the original 13 colonies.

DECLARATION OF INDEPENDENCE. Drafted by Thomas Jefferson, this document outlines the principles of independence, and includes the rights to "Life, Liberty, and the pursuit of Happiness."

A New Nation

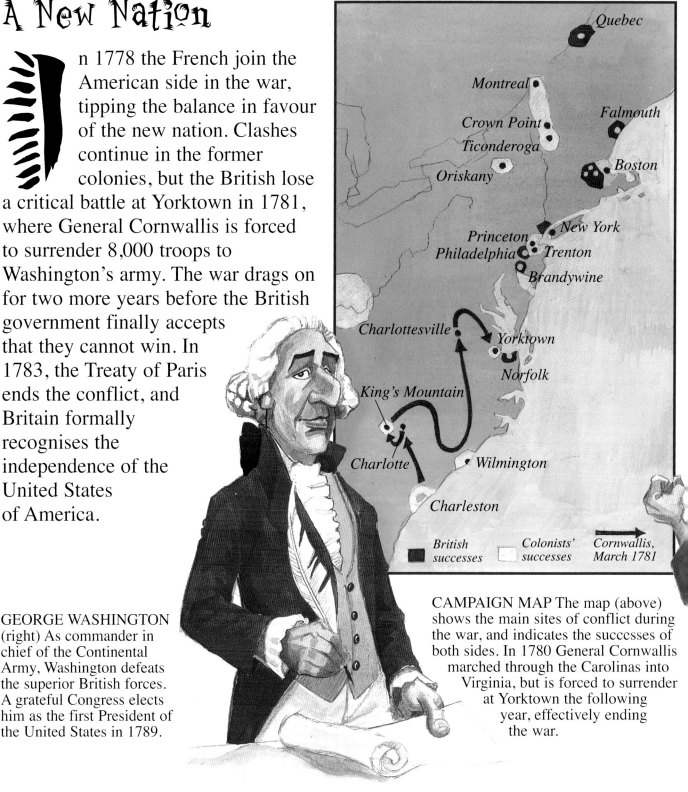

n 1778 the French join the American side in the war, tipping the balance in favour of the new nation. Clashes continue in the former colonies, but the British lose a critical battle at Yorktown in 1781, where General Cornwallis is forced to surrender 8,000 troops to Washington's army. The war drags on for two more years before the British government finally accepts that they cannot win. In 1783, the Treaty of Paris ends the conflict, and Britain formally recognises the independence of the United States of America.

GEORGE WASHINGTON (right) As commander in chief of the Continental Army, Washington defeats the superior British forces. A grateful Congress elects him as the first President of the United States in 1789.

Quebec
Montreal
Crown Point
Falmouth
Ticonderoga
Oriskany
Boston
Princeton
New York
Philadelphia
Trenton
Brandywine
Charlottesville
Yorktown
Norfolk
King's Mountain
Charlotte
Wilmington
Charleston

British successes
Colonists' successes
Cornwallis, March 1781

CAMPAIGN MAP The map (above) shows the main sites of conflict during the war, and indicates the successes of both sides. In 1780 General Cornwallis marched through the Carolinas into Virginia, but is forced to surrender at Yorktown the following year, effectively ending the war.

WHEN THE WAR ENDS you do not return to Boston as the British have burned down your shop. You and your wife move to a nearby town, where you will have 16 children. But the part you played on the night of December 16th, 1773, will not be forgotten. You live to the great age of 98 and become famous as one of the last living survivors of the Boston Tea Party.

Handy hint

Don't forget to celebrate Independence Day each year on July 4th!

THE CENTENARIAN (below).
Your portrait now hangs in the library of the Bostonian Society. It is wrongly called *The Centenarian* because it was believed at the time that you were over 100-years-old.

INDEPENDENCE DAY (above) You become a popular figure at Independence Day celebrations held on the Fourth of July.

Glossary

Brand A mark burned on the skin of a criminal as a punishment.

British East India Company A trading company that was chartered by the British government in 1600 to develop trade in Asia.

Centenarian A person who lives for 100 years.

Continental Congress The first government of the United States of America, formed in 1774.

Courier A person carrying messages.

Customs A duty or tax imposed on imported goods.

Debtor Someone who owes money to another person or company.

Handbill A printed document or pamphlet delivered by hand.

Liberty Tree An ancient elm on the corner of Essex Street and Orange Street in Boston. It was a focal point for anti-British meetings.

Lobster back A colonist's nickname for British soldiers, whose red coats were like the colour of boiled lobsters.

Loyalists American colonists who did not want independence from Britain.

Militia A military force composed of civilians who can be called upon for emergency service.

Mohawk A tribe of Indians native to the area that is now New York State.

Porphyria An inherited disease that can cause mental confusion.

Privateer A privately owned ship and its crew, who are authorised by a government to attack and capture enemy ships during wartime.

Quarters Housing for military personnel.

Sons of Liberty (also referred to as The Sons within the text). An organisation founded in November 1765 to oppose the Stamp Act.

Tar-and-feather A punishment in which a person's body is smeared with tar and then coated with feathers (which stick to the tar).

Tyranny Absolute power, especially when exercised unjustly or cruelly.

Whipping Post A post set up in a public place to which offenders are tied to be whipped.

Index